William Henry Hodgkins

The Battle of Fort Stedman

Petersburg, Virginia - March 25, 1865

William Henry Hodgkins

The Battle of Fort Stedman
Petersburg, Virginia - March 25, 1865

ISBN/EAN: 9783337748913

Printed in Europe, USA, Canada, Australia, Japan

Cover: Foto ©Andreas Hilbeck / pixelio.de

More available books at **www.hansebooks.com**

THE

BATTLE OF FORT STEDMAN

(PETERSBURG, VIRGINIA)

MARCH 25, 1865

BY

WILLIAM H. HODGKINS

Thirty-sixth Regiment Massachusetts Volunteers; Brevet Major U.S. Vols.; Staff of Third Division Ninth Army Corps

BOSTON
PRIVATELY PRINTED
1889

INTRODUCTORY.

THE following narrative, which was originally prepared for publication as a magazine article, has far exceeded the ordinary limits of such a paper, and is now printed as one more, though slight, contribution to the "Literature of the Civil War." The writer served on the Staff of General John F. Hartranft, Commanding Third Division, Ninth Army Corps, and was a witness to, and participant in, the battle. In addition to very full private data, he has had access to several reports not yet printed. He acknowledges his obligation to Generals Parke, Hartranft, Willcox, and Tidball for very valuable information relating to the battle; and especial thanks to Comrade Francis W. Knowles (Company B, Thirty-sixth Massachusetts Volunteers), Chief Clerk at General Willcox's (First) Division Headquarters, for a drawing of the valuable map which accompanies this narrative, and for interesting details from his personal diary and retained copies of papers.

PETERSBURG.

Long years have swiftly passed away,
  In Time's unceasing flight,
Since last I saw those fields of woe,
  Where Wrong resisted Right.
   .   .   .   .   .   .

The pulse is quickened, and the brain
  With recollection teems,
Of sad and tenderest memories,
  Like some forgotten dreams.

Once more I see the busy camps,
  With white tents far and near;
Long vanished scenes, familiar sounds,
  Again greet eye and ear.
I hear the squadron's measured tramp,
  I see the bayonet's glare:
The music of the fife and drum
  Comes floating in the air.

The sentry's beat, the picket post,
  The skirmishers I see,
The battle line, the thrilling charge —
  Hear cheers of victory.
   .   .   .   .   .

But all is calm and peaceful now
  On those historic lines,
And sadly blows the Southern wind,
  Sweet-scented with the pines;
Chanting a solemn requiem
  O'er slumbers most profound
Of those who fell and sweetly sleep
  In consecrated ground.
   .   .   .   .   .   .

HON. J. W. MORRISON,
100th Regiment, Pennsylvania Volunteers.

THE BATTLE OF FORT STEDMAN.

THE event known in the history of the Rebellion as the "Battle of Fort Stedman," which was fought March 25, 1865, in the lines near Petersburg, Virginia, has received at the hand of the general historian only brief and inadequate notice. This is owing in a large degree doubtless to the fact that the momentous events attending the final campaign of the armies under General Grant's immediate command, beginning only four days later, which resulted in the destruction of the Army of Northern Virginia and the downfall of the Confederacy, have overshadowed in the public mind the brilliant engagement at Fort Stedman. It has been regarded simply as an episode, — a bold dash upon, and speedy recovery of, a line of entrenchments, having no special significance, and but little direct or material bearing, upon the campaign which followed.

Whatever may be the verdict of history upon this point, the fact remains that, considering the numbers of the troops that took part in it, it was one of the most important engagements of the late war, and fully attained to the dignity of a battle. Had it occurred during any other campaign or at any other period, or as an isolated

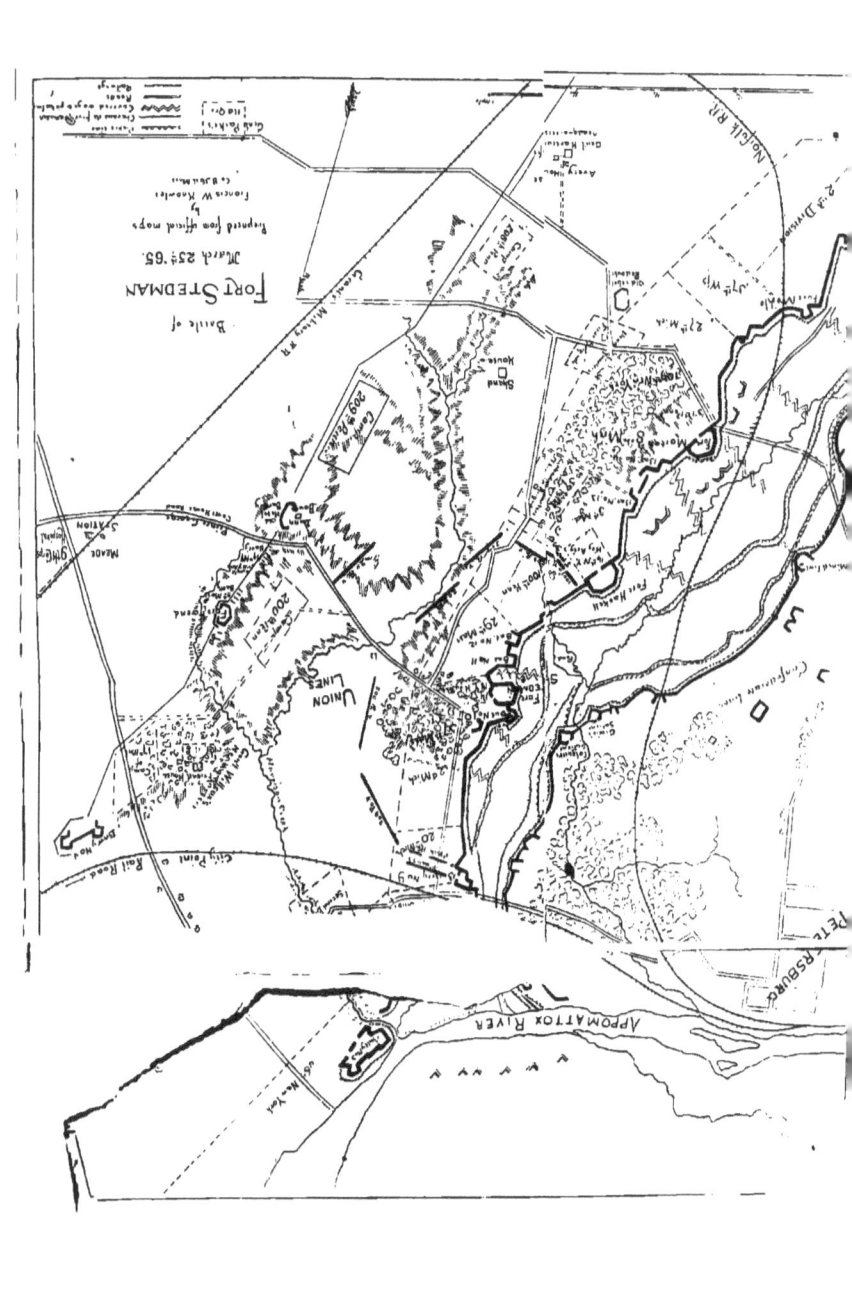

event in the long siege of Petersburg, it would have ac-
quired prominence in the annals of the war.

It was the last desperate thrust of the Army of Northern Virginia before the agonies of its dissolution ; and as
a fair offset to the disaster which befel the Ninth Army
Corps at the battle of the Mine in the same locality
eight months previous, it is worthy of extended description, and to a more prominent position in history than it
has yet attained.

In Union histories and reports this interesting action
is known as the " Battle of Fort Stedman " (though often
erroneously called " Steedman " and " Steadman "), while
in Confederate accounts it is designated the " Battle of
Hare's Hill."

Fort Stedman was situated on Hare's Hill, two miles
from the centre of Petersburg, at the point where the
Union entrenchments crossed the Prince George Court-
house road. It formed a part of the Confederate position
which was captured by the troops of the Second Corps
in the general assault on the evening of June 16, 1864.
It was named in honor of Colonel Griffin A. Stedman,
of Hartford, Connecticut, Colonel of the Eleventh Regiment Connecticut Volunteers, Brevet Brigadier-General
U.S.V.   He commanded a Brigade in Martindale's
(Second) Division, Eighteenth Army Corps, and was
actively engaged in the attacks upon the defences of
Petersburg, June 15–18, 1864. On the 18th of June,
after three days of fighting, his brigade occupied the

extreme right of the Union lines stretching from the Appomattox river on the right to a point near the Petersburg and City Point Railroad on the left. The gallant conduct of the brigade and its commander elicited merited praise. On the 21st of June the Second Corps, which had occupied a position between the Eighteenth and Ninth Corps, was withdrawn, and the ground vacated was occupied by the Eighteenth Corps extending to the left, and the Ninth Corps to the right. Colonel Stedman's Brigade held the line at Hare's Hill, connecting with the Ninth Corps. It is a singular coincidence that the extension of these corps united temporarily the troops of the old Ninth Corps, which had been separated since March, 1863, when the then Third Division, in which was the Eleventh Connecticut, was sent to Suffolk, Virginia, and ultimately joined the Eighteenth Corps, while the First and Second Divisions were transferred, with their commander, General Burnside, to the Department of the Ohio, and subsequently to the Army of the Potomac.

Colonel Stedman was mortally wounded on the 5th of August, 1864, and died the following day. In commemoration of his gallant services the fort at this point received his name.

It occupied the main eminence of the ridge. On its immediate left was Battery Eleven, a small ravelin for two guns. From the left of this battery extended a curtain which connected it with Battery Twelve, a nearly square

redoubt mounting four Cochorn mortars. To the left of
Battery Twelve, on high ground, about three-eighths of a
mile from Fort Stedman, was Fort Haskell, a strong forti-
fication mounting six guns, besides mortars. The pan
coupé[1] of Battery Eleven was nearly on the crest of a
ridge which, on the one side, was the water-shed of Harri-
son's creek within our lines, and on the other was the
water-shed of a creek flowing through the enemy's lines,
but obstructed by them, and forming a pond in front of
and to the left of Battery Eleven. This last creek was
formed of two confluents, at a point near our picket lines, —
one flowing through the railroad culvert from the enemy's
side, the other through our lines to the left of Battery
Eleven, these two branches both rising from opposite sides
of the same hill, on which stood Fort Haskell.

Fort Stedman was projected as a salient toward the
Confederate lines. It was a comparatively small work
without bastions, covering about three-fourths of an acre
of ground. In the fort and around it, in rear, was a
grove of large shade-trees which had been allowed to re-
main. The fort had formed a part of the enemy's defences, and, like all our position on this portion of the
lines, was originally gained by our troops under fire. It
was not compactly built in the first place, and had been
considerably weakened by frosts and storms, and the parapet had greatly settled during the winter. Its nearness

---

[1] Pan coupé — The short length of parapet by which the salient angle of a work
is sometimes cut off. (Mil. dictionary.)

to the enemy prevented even the slightest repairs except
in the most stealthy manner, as any attempt to strengthen
it was stoutly resisted. The fort had a comparatively
small line of infantry parapet, particularly in front,
which was cut with embrasures for artillery. It was protected in front by abatis and various obstructions.

On its immediate right, and forming almost a part of
the fort itself, was Battery Ten, an open work, mounting
four guns. Next in the line was Battery Nine. On the
right the hill declined rapidly toward the plain, and the
ground was low and wet. The position at this point combined many disadvantages. The frequent rains rendered
the hollow very muddy, and the underground bomb-proofs
were more or less full of water continually. The works
were in an incomplete state, owing to the unfavorable nature of the ground and the exposure to a most annoying
and constant picket fire which rendered it very unsafe to
traverse the lines. A line of parapet connected Battery
Nine with Battery Eight and Fort McGilvery, the first
fort on the left of the Appomattox. Fort Stedman was
distant from the river about seven-eighths of a mile, and
from the Friend House about one mile and a half. Meade
Station, the nearest point on the military railroad, was
one mile in rear.

On the continuation of the ridge upon which Fort Stedman stood, towards Petersburg, was located the strongly
fortified position of the enemy at Spring Hill, called Colquitt's Salient. The batteries in and around this position

mounted twenty guns of various calibres. A formidable
triple row of *chevaux-de-frise* protected it from assault.
In rear was a road twenty feet wide, in a broad deep
ravine, in which great numbers of troops could be massed;
and the road was continued as a completely covered way
as far as Blandford, a suburb of Petersburg. To the right
of Stedman and to the left of Colquitt's the lines receded
from each other, the race-course lying between them. It
will be seen that the salients and posts of honor at this
portion of the lines were Colquitt's Salient and Batteries,
Fort Stedman, and Batteries Eleven and Twelve. An attack to the right of Stedman would expose troops to an
enfilading fire on the plain; to the left of Stedman, to the
difficulties of watercourses and ravines.[1] The distance
from Battery Ten to the point of the enemy's line (Colquitt's Salient), immediately opposite, was only six hundred and thirteen feet between the main works, the shortest
distance between the two at any point, excepting at Elli-
ott's Salient (the locality of the Mine). The picket lines
were only four hundred and thirty-five feet apart; those of
the enemy being only a few feet in front of his main
works; one of the Union pickets was separated only two
hundred and five feet from his opposite neighbor. General Grimes, who afterward led the assault on Fort Sted-

---

[1] For a portion of this description of the locality the writer is indebted to the report of Colonel Thos. Wm. Clarke, Twenty-ninth Regiment, Massachusetts Vols.,
to the Adjutant-General of the State, 1865. Colonel Clarke was A.A.A.G. of the
brigade occupying this ground.

man, in a letter to his family, says the lines "are so close that you can almost see the whites of the Yankees' eyes."[1]

The crest upon which Stedman stood was commanded in the immediate rear by two hills of nearly equal height, —the Dunn House hill, seven-eighths of a mile distant, on which stood the Dunn House Battery and Fort Friend; and the Friend House hill, one mile and a quarter distant, a little east of north. Both these hills were partly fortified, and artillery covered the rear and flanks. Between these hills and the main line were several detached, deserted works which had been thrown up by both armies during the early battles around Petersburg; these had been left standing by the Union Army, and, as we shall see, were destined to play a conspicuous part in the Battle of Fort Stedman.

On the 29th of November, 1864, the Ninth Army Corps was ordered from its camp near Peeble's Farm, on the left of the army, where it had been located during the autumn, and marched to the right, to occupy its former position in the blood-stained trenches fronting the city of Petersburg. The First Division, Brevet Major-General O. B. Willcox, commanding, was placed on the extreme right, and occupied the trenches from the Appomattox river to Fort Meikle. The Second Division, Brevet Major-General R. B. Potter, commanding, extended the line from that point to Fort Howard, — the two divisions

---

[1] Extracts of letters of Major-General Bryan Grimes to his wife. Raleigh, N. C., 1884, page 98.

covering a front of more than seven miles. The three brigades of the First Division were disposed as follows:

The Second, Colonel Ralph Ely, commanding, held the right from the river to near Battery Nine; the Third, Brevet Brigadier-General N. B. McLaughlin, commanding, from Battery Nine to the left of Fort Haskell; the First, Colonel Samuel Harriman, Thirty-seventh Wisconsin Volunteers, commanding, from that point to Fort Meikle. The front covered by this division was more than three miles in length.

The Third Division, composed of six new regiments of Pennsylvania Volunteers, commanded by Brigadier-General John F. Hartranft, was in reserve,—a brigade in rear of each division in the trenches. His headquarters were at the Avery House. His regiments were encamped as follows: Two Hundredth Regiment, Lieutenant-Colonel William H. H. McCall, commanding, near the Dunn House Battery; Two Hundred and Ninth Regiment, Lieutenant-Colonel George W. Frederick, commanding, on the high ground near Meade Station; Two Hundred and Eighth Regiment, Colonel A. B. McCalmont, commanding, near the Avery House. These regiments constituted the First Brigade, commanded by Colonel Charles W. Diven, Two Hundredth Regiment. The Second Brigade, Colonel Joseph A. Mathews, Two Hundred and Fifth Regiment, commanding,—comprising the Two Hundred and Fifth, Major B. M. Morrow, commanding, Two Hundred and Seventh, Colonel Robert C. Cox, commanding, and

Two Hundred and Eleventh Regiments, Captain William A. Coulter, commanding,— lay in rear of the Second Division line between Forts Alexander Hays and Howard,— the latter regiment being posted near Fort Prescott.

The Artillery of the Ninth Corps was commanded by Brevet Brigadier-General John C. Tidball. The Reserve Artillery was camped near Meade Station.

The Ninth Corps was ably commanded by Major-General John G. Parke, whose headquarters were about one mile from the Avery House.

Forts Stedman and Haskell were garrisoned by detachments of the Fourteenth New York Heavy Artillery, Major George M. Randall, commanding, acting as infantry. The mortar batteries in all that portion of the lines were manned by the First Connecticut Heavy Artillery. The Light Artillery and mortars from Battery Nine to Fort Haskell were stationed as follows:—

Battery Nine, two light twelves; Batteries C and I, Fifth United States Artillery, Capt. Valentine H. Stone, and two Coehorn mortars, Lieut. Azro Drown; Battery Ten, two 3-inch rifles, Fourteenth Massachusetts Light Artillery, Lieut. Ephraim B. Nye, and three Coehorns and four 8-inch mortars, Capt. Jno. M. Twiss and Lieut. Jno. Odell; Fort Stedman, four light twelves of Nineteenth New York Light Battery, Capt. Edward W. Rogers; Battery Twelve, four Coehorns and two 8-inch mortars, Lieut. Robert Lewis; Fort Haskell, four light

twelves of Third New Jersey Light Battery, Brevet-
Major Christian Woerner, and four Coehorns, Lieut. W.
H. H. Bingham.

The Thirty-fourth New York Light Battery, Brevet-
Major Jacob Roemer, commanding, had been stationed in
Fort Friend, in rear of Fort Stedman, but on the evening
of March 24th was placed in Fort McGilvery, exchanging
positions with the Eleventh Massachusetts Light Battery,
Brevet-Major Edward J. Jones, commanding.

The winter of 1864–5 had been severe and trying to the
waning fortunes of the Confederacy. General Sheridan's
successes had ended the campaign in the Shenandoah
Valley, and the armies had been withdrawn from it.
General Hood had been overwhelmed, and his army
scattered by the victory attending the campaign of General Thomas in front of Nashville; and ever and anon
tidings of the onward and' victorious march of General
Sherman's army had been heralded to the Army of
Northern Virginia in double-shotted salutes of one hundred cannon, as one after the other, in quick succession,
—Savannah, Charleston, Columbia, and Wilmington,—
had fallen.

That commander was then closing around the army
of General Johnston in North Carolina, preparatory to
the final struggle. The outlook was dark and foreboding.
The number of deserters from General Lee's army in-
creased daily. The return of spring was to usher in a
great campaign. The trains sent to the left were filled

with supplies and troops, as General Grant continued to mass heavily in the direction of Lee's right. To the soldiers of Lee's army the rumble of these heavily loaded trains was like the muttering of thunder before the bursting of the storm.

As the season for active operations drew near, General Grant became uneasy. General Badeau says: "Grant had now spent many days of anxiety lest each morning should bring the news that the enemy had retreated the night before. He was firmly convinced that the crossing of the Roanoke by Sherman would be the signal for Lee to leave; and if Johnston and Lee were combined, a long and tedious and expensive campaign, consuming most of the summer, might be inevitable. His anxiety was well founded, for during Sherman's delay the rebel commanders were conferring in order to effect a junction."

Accordingly, on the 24th of March, only the day before the action we are about to notice, he had issued orders for a general movement to the left on the 29th, with the purpose to destroy the Danville and the Southside railroads, turn Lee's right, and force him to abandon his entrenchments.

Jefferson Davis says:[1] "In the early part of March, . . . General Lee held with me a long and free conference. Is stated that the circumstances had forced on him the conclusion that the evacuation of Petersburg was but

---

[1] The Rise and Fall of the Confederate Government, Vol. II., p. 648, *et seq.*

a question of time. . . . To my inquiry whether it would not be better to anticipate the necessity by withdrawing at once, he said that his artillery and draught horses were too weak for the roads in their then condition, and that he would have to wait until they became firmer. . . . The programme was to retire to Danville, at which place supplies should be collected and a junction made with the troops of General Johnston, the combined force to be hurled upon Sherman in North Carolina, with the hope of defeating him before Grant could come to his relief. . . . General Lee was averse to retiring from his enemy. He had so often beaten superior numbers, that his thoughts were no doubt directed to every possible expedient which might enable him to avoid retreat. It thus fell out that, in a week or two after the conference above noticed, he presented to me the idea of a sortie against the enemy near to the right of his line. This was rendered the more feasible, from the constant extension of Grant's line to the left, and the heavy bodies of troops he was employing to turn our right. The sortie, if entirely successful, so as to capture and hold the works on Grant's right, as well as three forts on the commanding ridge in his rear, would threaten his line of communication with his base, City Point, and compel him to move his forces around ours to protect it; if only so far successful as to cause the transfer of his troops from his left to his right, it would relieve our right, and delay the impending disaster for the more convenient season for retreat."

A sortie against Fort Stedman having been decided upon, Mr. Davis continues: "For this service, requiring equal daring and steadiness, General John B. Gordon, well proved on many battle-fields, was selected. His command was the remnant of Ewell's Corps, troops often tried in the fiery ordeal of battle, and always found true as tempered steel." This was the "Stonewall" Jackson Corps, which had been recently withdrawn from the Shenandoah Valley, and posted on the right of General Lee's army. On the 10th of March this corps was transferred to the trenches around Petersburg, for the purpose, as General Gordon states,[1] of enabling him to carefully examine the lines and report to General Lee the practicability of breaking them at any point. He says: "Within a week after being transferred to this new position, I decided that Fort Stedman could be taken by a night assault, and that it might be possible to throw into the breach thus made in Grant's lines a sufficient force to disorganize and destroy the left wing of his army before he could recover and concentrate his forces, then lying between the James and Appomattox rivers.

"General Lee, after considering the plan of assault and battle which I submitted to him, and which I shall presently describe, gave me orders to prepare for the movement, which was regarded by both of us as a desperate one, but which seemed to give more promise of good results than any other hitherto suggested. General Lee

---

[1] The Rise and Fall of the Confederate Government, page 650.

placed at my disposal, in addition to my own corps, a portion of A. P. Hill's and a portion of Longstreet's, and a detachment of cavalry, — in all, about one-half of the army.

"The general plan of the assault and battle was this: To take the fort [Stedman] by a rush across the narrow space that lay between it and Colquitt's Salient, and then surprise and capture, by a stratagem, the commanding forts in the rear, thus opening a way for our troops to pass to the rear, and upon the flank of the left wing of Grant's army, which was to be broken to pieces by a concentration of all the forces at my command moving upon the flank. During the night of the 24th my preparations were made for the movement before daylight. I placed three officers in charge of three separate bodies of men, and directed them, as soon as the lines of Fort Stedman should be carried by the assaulting column, to rush through the gap thus produced to the three rear forts, — one of these officers and bodies to go to each fort, and to approach them from their rear, by the only avenue left open, and seize those forts. A guide was placed with each of these officers, who was to conduct him and his troops to the rear of the front [fort?], which he was to surprise. A body of the most stalwart of my men was organized to move in advance of all the troops, armed with axes, with which they were to cut down the obstruction of sharpened and wire-fastened rails in front of the enemy's lines.

"Next to these were to come three hundred men, armed

with bayonets fixed and empty muskets, who were to mount and enter the fort as the axe-men cut away the obstruction of sharpened rails, bayoneting the pickets in front and gunners in the fort if they resisted, or sending them to our rear if they surrendered. Next were to cross the three officers and their detachments, who were to capture the three rear forts. Next, a division of infantry was to cross, moving by the left flank, so as to be in position, when halted and fronted, to move without any confusion or delay immediately down General Grant's lines, toward his left, capturing his troops, or forcing them to abandon their works and form under our advancing fire at right angles to his line of works.

"Next was to cross the cavalry, who were to ride to the rear, cut the enemy's telegraph lines, capture his pontoons, and prevent or delay the crossing of reinforcements from beyond the Appomattox. Next, my whole force was to swell the column of attack. Then, as the front of our lines was cleared of the enemy's troops, our divisions were to change front and join in pressing upon the enemy, driving him farther from the other wing of General Grant's army, and widening the breach."

At a Council of War, in which the question of making an offensive movement and the capture of the opposing fort by a storming party was discussed, and the duties of the various officers assigned, a high tribute was paid to the courage of the Louisiana brigades.

"'On account of the valor of your troops,' said

General Evans to Colonel Waggaman, 'you will be allowed the honor of leading off in the attack.' This you will make with unloaded muskets.' At three o'clock in the morning, Waggaman, who had been watching all night, silently awakened his men and moved forward outside of the breastworks. In so doing his command, during the darkness and confusion, was cut in two by the marching of other Confederate commands. He passed out through Gracie's Salient to the objective point of the Federal works, and the key of the position, towards the guns of Fort Stedman." [2]

The picket officer of McLaughlin's Brigade, Captain John F. Burch, Third Maryland Volunteers, reports that he visited the picket line at four o'clock on the morning of March 25, and found the men wakeful and on the alert, after which he returned to his quarters in front of Fort Stedman. He states that, a few minutes after his return, a man on the lookout gave notice that the enemy were approaching, and at the same time the men on the post fired their muskets. Major Charles T. Richardson, the commanding officer of the Twenty-ninth Massachusetts Volunteers, on duty at Battery Eleven, states: "Existing orders from army headquarters encouraged the enemy to

---

[1] Military Annals of Louisiana. New Orleans, 1875, page 39 *et seq.*

[2] These brigades, consisting of ten Louisiana regiments, composed two brigades, formerly known as Hays's and Stafford's Brigades. They were united under General York, and were, at the time under review, commanded by Colonel Eugene Waggaman, Tenth Louisiana, and the former title, "Louisiana Brigades," retained.

desert, and offered them payment for arms brought across;" and " the multitude of deserters from the enemy, coming peaceably with arms, had caused some carelessness in this regard. On the morning of the 25th of March, deserters began, about three o'clock, to come across in considerable numbers, — too large to send guards with from the picket line, so that the officer of the guard directed them retained on the picket line, and roused the troops in Fort Stedman, sending word to Battery Eleven to be on the alert, as matters looked suspicious."[1] These pretended deserters gained possession of the picket line in overpowering numbers. They proved to be the skirmishers of the enemy, and were closely followed by the strong storming party of picked men ; this by the heavy columns referred to by General Gordon. The enemy advanced in three columns, — one toward the left of Battery Ten ; the second, to a point between Fort Stedman and Battery Eleven ; and a third, direct toward Fort Stedman. It is estimated that there were more than eight thousand men in these columns. The guard, though stoutly resisting, was unable to withstand this force. The enemy's left column was the first to break through, and soon gained Battery Ten. Here, as has been stated, were stationed two guns of the Fourteenth Massachusetts Light Battery, Lieutenant Nye, commanding, and a detachment of the First Connecticut Heavy Artillery, commanded by Captain Twiss, in charge of the mortars. No alarm had been

---

[1] Massachusetts Adjutant-General's Report, 1865, pp. 403-4.

given here, and the assault was so sudden, that but one
round was fired from each gun. It was so dark that foe
could not be distinguished from friend, and at one time
the enemy were firing a part of the guns and our men the
others. The firing revealed the position of our men, and
the cannoniers were immediately seized and thrown over
the works into the ditch.[1] Captain Twiss of the Mortars
was wounded, Lieutenants Nye of the Artillery and Odell
of the Mortars were killed at the guns, and most of the
garrison were killed or wounded or captured. In the darkness and confusion several of the cannoniers made their
escape to the Reserve Camp at Meade Station. The capture of Battery Ten gave the enemy a wide opening on the
right and rear, and great advantage over Stedman, the
ground just in rear being on a level with the parapet of
the Fort, and they entered the sally-port almost undiscovered. From the four light twelve-pound guns a dozen
rounds of canister were discharged into the enemy's ranks,
and the battalion of the Fourteenth New York Heavy
Artillery, under Major Randall, made a stubborn resistance ;
but, being attacked in front, flank, and rear, was speedily
overpowered and most of them captured.[2] The situation was fearful for several moments. As the enemy
jumped into the enclosure where the defenders were now
awake and stirring, such was the excitement and desperate

---

[1] Report of Fourteenth Light Battery.   Massachusetts Adjutant-General's
Report for 1865, page 757.

[2] Major Randall, with the regimental colors, made his escape, passed to the left
among the works, and joined a battalion of his regiment in Fort Haskell.

energy of the struggle, that the combatants fought, as was afterwards said, "as if they had drank two quarts of brandy." The fort was finally carried, though it was rough-and-tumble fighting ; the opposing soldiers being locked together like serpents. As defendants refused to surrender, they were knocked in the head with the musket or bayoneted by the assailants.[1] The guns in the Fort and Battery Ten were at once turned against the troops in our lines, and the enemy pushed along the entrenchments to Battery Eleven, where the Twenty-ninth Massachusetts was encountered. Upon the sound of the firing this regiment had been aroused, and took its position in the line ; but the firing was so slight that, when the command was given to "fall in," the sentinel on the top of the parapet called out that there was "no attack." The pickets of this regiment could be seen standing quietly by their fires in the ravine below, apparently unaware that an attack had been made on the main line. Up to this time no general alarm had been sounded, and at this point there was no indication that the line had been broken, or that danger lurked in the rear. Suddenly the men in the right curtain commenced firing ; they were ordered to cease, lest they should shoot their own pickets, who had begun to come in. The latter order had hardly been given when Gordon's troops suddenly appeared in the rear.[2] A des-

---

1 Military Annals of Louisiana.

2 History of Twenty-ninth Regiment, Massachusetts Volunteers, page 328 *et seq.* There are discrepancies and contradictions in the published reports and histories

perate hand-to-hand fight continued for fifteen minutes ;
and after a very severe struggle, during which the regiment
displayed staying qualities of a high order, and captured
nearly twice as many prisoners as it numbered, the enemy
succeeded in driving it out of the battery, capturing nearly
all the defenders, while the remainder formed a line in the
rear, partially closing the gap, and word was sent to brigade
headquarters of the condition of affairs in Battery Eleven.
The Brigade Commander, General McLaughlin, on hearing the firing, sent his staff to various portions of the line,
and went himself to Fort Haskell, finding the troops there
on the alert, ready to resist an attack.   He then turned
down the line to the right, passing the One Hundredth
Pennsylvania, already in the works, and Battery Twelve,
toward Battery Eleven, where he was informed by the
commanding officer of the Twenty-ninth Massachusetts
that the battery had been taken and his regiment just
driven out.   He sent orders at once to the Fifty-ninth
Massachusetts, a reserve regiment near his headquarters,
and the only regiment of his brigade not in the lines, to
report on the double-quick, and also ordered the mortars
in Battery Twelve to be turned on Battery Eleven.   As
soon as the Fifty-ninth Massachusetts arrived, he ordered
it and the remnant of the Twenty-ninth Massachusetts to
charge with fixed bayonets, and they recaptured Battery
Eleven at once.   Supposing he had restored the only break

of this affair. Where these conflict with the manuscript report of the brigade
commander, the latter has been regarded as authority.

in his lines, he crossed the parapet into Stedman, and meeting some men coming over the curtains, whom in the darkness he supposed to be his own men, he established them inside the fort, and gave directions about firing, which were instantly obeyed. In a few moments he saw a man crossing the parapet whose uniform in the dawning light he recognized to be the enemy's. He halted him, to ascertain what regiment he belonged to. This called attention to himself, and in a moment he was surrounded by the enemy, whom he had supposed to be his own men, and was sent across the lines and conducted to General Gordon, to whom he surrendered his sword, and was then taken to Petersburg. While he was standing by General Gordon, four brigades of the enemy moved forward to our works.[1] About this time Brevet-Major Henry L. Swords, Division Staff Officer of the day, was sent by General Willcox to General McLaughlin with orders. He went at once to Fort Haskell, but not finding him, galloped along the line of works, then deserted, to Fort Stedman, and upon attempting to enter rode into a mass of struggling, fighting men crowding out from the fort. They proved to be the enemy, and he was taken prisoner and sent across the parapet, where he also met General Gordon, and was afterward taken to Petersburg.[2]

The enemy's left column turned to our right down the works toward Battery Nine, striking the flank of the Fifty-

---

[1] General McLaughlin's manuscript report.

[2] Letter of Major Swords to the writer.

seventh Massachusetts, capturing a portion, and driving out
the remainder, who retired out of reach of the fire, and,
as we shall see, did good service afterwards. The Second
Michigan was next encountered, but as this regiment had
received warning, it was able to fight the enemy on this
flank in a most spirited manner from their bomb-proofs and
traverses. By order of Colonel Ely, brigade commander,
the regiment was drawn into Battery Nine, which, though
small, was an enclosed work. The artillery in Battery
Nine opened a heavy fire upon the enemy's flank, and
Colonel Ely hurried the First Michigan Sharp-shooters
from his right and formed it at right angles with the line
of entrenchments, where they fought with such success as
to prevent any farther advance of the enemy in that
direction, and the line of trenches vacated by the Second
Michigan was for a considerable time unoccupied by either
party.[1]   .

While these startling events were happening on the
front line, active and important movements were taking
place in rear, which were destined to stem the tide of disaster and wrest victory from confusion and defeat.

As nearly as can be determined from reports, despatches,
and observation, the three commanders, Generals Parke,

---

[1] Lieutenant-Colonel Monier, commanding Tenth Louisiana, in his diary
(published in " Military Annals of Louisiana "), after describing assault on Fort
Stedman, says: " An advance is now made toward Battery Number Five, and ar-
rive within three hundred yards of it. Here the confident progress was arrested
by large reinforcements reaching the enemy." The corps of sharpshooters of the
Louisiana brigade led the attacking column.

Willcox, and Hartranft, were made aware of the assault at about the same moment of time. They were immediately on the alert, and, comprehending the situation of affairs, took such active measures as were deemed necessary to expel the enemy and restore the breach in the lines. General Willcox, as we have seen, despatched a staff officer to Fort Stedman, and communicated with his brigade commanders. General Parke at once directed Brigadier-General Tidball, Chief of Artillery, to occupy all available ground with the Reserve Artillery, ordered General Willcox to reoccupy the works taken, and General Hartranft to concentrate his division and reinforce General Willcox.

He immediately telegraphed the condition of affairs to the Army of the Potomac headquarters, but receiving no reply, telegraphed again and again, with like result. In reply to his *fourth* despatch he was informed that General Meade was not at headquarters, and that the command of the army devolved upon himself. This was the first intimation he had received of the absence of General Meade, who was at City Point, in conference with General Grant. It being reported to General Parke that telegraphic communication with City Point was interrupted, he at once despatched a courier to that place to announce the state of affairs to Generals Grant and Meade.

As we have already noticed, General Hartranft had two regiments encamped near the scene of the attack: the Two Hundredth Pennsylvania, near the Dunn House Battery, and the Two Hundred and Ninth, at Meade Station.

It being understood by Generals Willcox and Hartranft that, in case of an attack, in order to avoid delay in communicating first with General Hartranft, owing to the great length of line covered by his command, the former should order these regiments wherever they might be needed in his line, General Willcox now sent orders for these regiments to move at once, — the Two Hundredth to the front of the Dunn House Battery, the Two Hundred and Ninth to the Friend House Hill. Meantime the enemy's skirmishers began to advance down the hill directly in rear of Fort Stedman, moving towards General Wilcox's headquarters at the Friend House, the Dunn House Battery, and Meade Station; and General Wilcox ordered out the Seventeenth Michigan, a small regiment detailed as engineers at his headquarters, for duty as skirmishers.

Immediately upon hearing the alarm and the firing on the right, General Hartranft sent Captain Dalien of his staff from headquarters at the Avery House to General McLaughlin's to ascertain the cause of the alarm, and at the same time Colonels Diven and Mathews, his brigade commanders, were ordered to place their commands under arms ready for any emergency. Captain Dalien soon returned with a message from General McLaughlin's adjutant-general,[1] stating that "the enemy had carried the lines from Battery Eleven and Stedman to the right, and were moving toward the river." Within a few minutes he received an order from General Parke to "move his First

---

[1] Colonel Thomas Wm. Clarke.

Brigade to reinforce General Willcox, in order to re-capture a Battery reported to be captured near Fort Stedman."

He at once started in person to the right, and at the same time ordered the Two Hundred and Eighth Regiment to report immediately to General McLaughlin. He then proceeded to General Willcox's headquarters, arriving just as his two regiments, which had been ordered out by General Willcox, were moving toward the points designated by the latter. He found General Willcox, with his staff mounted, baggage packed, and headquarters tents struck, ready for a movement to the rear. He immediately assumed personal supervision over his own command. General Hartranft says: "While talking with General Willcox, our attention was called to the puffs of smoke issuing from the wood in the rear, and to the right and left of Fort Stedman. It was not yet light enough to see the enemy, nor could any sound be heard, owing to the direction of the wind, but the white puffs indicated musketry firing." Being satisfied that this was an attack in force, and that time must be gained at any cost, General Hartranft determined at once to force the fighting, and not wait for the remainder of his troops to come up. At his request General Willcox detailed one of his staff officers, Brevet-Major L. Curtis Brackett, Fifty-seventh Massachusetts Volunteers, to lead the Two Hundred and Ninth Regiment by the flank down the road to the left of the Friend House, while he himself took the Two Hundredth Regiment, which was nearest at

hand, to check the enemy, who were advancing with a
heavy line of skirmishers, followed by an assaulting
column or a line of battle, from the rear of Fort Stedman
towards the ravine, and covering the main road leading to
Meade Station and the Ninth Corps hospitals.[1] General
Hartranft found a small detachment of the Fifty-seventh
Massachusetts in command of a captain (which, as we
have seen, were driven out of their camp), deployed as
skirmishers just in front of the Two Hundredth Regiment.
It was at once ordered back to its camp, and the Two
Hundredth followed to that point without serious loss,
though under a sharp fire. Without losing any time in
feeling the enemy or fighting his skirmishers, the Two
Hundredth Regiment advanced in line of battle, breaking
the enemy's line of skirmishers, and driving in those
directly in front; but in the road leading to Meade
Station, and in some old works beyond the road on our
left, the line was strong and the enemy in force, and the
guns of Stedman, just captured and turned against the
Union line, were on the right. General Hartranft sent

---

[1] General Grimes, commanding Gordon's Advance Division, says: " This
morning [March 25] we charged the enemy's works and captured them, taking
twelve to fifteen pieces of artillery and a good many prisoners. . . . As
usual, I captured a horse to ride during the fight, as I could not get mine over the
breastworks. It would have done your heart good to hear the men cheer as I
rode up and down the line urging them to do their duty." (Extracts of letters of
Major-General Bryan Grimes, page 98.)

The horse referred to probably belonged to Major Randall. The artillery
was taken by being run over; the pieces were not removed from the line, but
were recaptured later.

Major Shorkley of his staff to bring up the Two Hundred
and Ninth Pennsylvania from the ravine on the right,
where it was partially hidden from the enemy's view and
sheltered from his fire, his intention being to place this
regiment on the right of his line. Without waiting for
its arrival, he immediately attacked with the Two Hundredth Regiment; but finding the enemy too strong to
be pushed, and the fire from the line and Stedman very
severe, and the right suffering very badly, he was obliged
to retire through the camp of the Fifty-seventh Massachusetts, and take shelter in an old line of works about forty
yards in its rear and toward the right. General Hartranft
says: "From horseback at this point, the enemy's officers
could now be plainly seen urging their men through Fort
Stedman, and endeavoring to deploy them in rear."
Fearful that the enemy seeing him withdraw the Two
Hundredth Regiment would attack him, General Hartranft immediately led the regiment forward and attacked
the second time. It promptly responded, and in the face
of a galling fire in front and flanks it succeeded in gaining
a commanding position where he could inflict some dam-
age on the enemy. The advance of this regiment was
gallant in the extreme. It was, like all of Hartranft's
troops, a new regiment, for the first time under direct fire,
and it was subjected to the severest test. It maintained
its ground gallantly for more than twenty minutes against
overwhelming odds, losing at this point more than one
hundred men, but gaining invaluable time. The regiment

became so shattered under the murderous fire that General Hartranft ordered it to retire, and it fell back in good
order to, and was again rallied in, the old line of works
from which it had advanced a second time. The Two
Hundred and Ninth Regiment, after strong opposition
and considerable loss, had now pushed its way to his
aid, and was placed by General Hartranft on his right,
which was still farther extended by the deployment of
the Seventeenth Michigan, prolonging his right to the
Second Michigan near Battery Nine, which, as stated, had
been reinforced and was now firmly held. With the aid
of the Artillery in Battery Nine, and the two Michigan
regiments of the First Division, he now had a strong line
which would prevent any advance of the enemy in that
direction. Seeing that he could accomplish nothing more
with the force then in hand, and being fully satisfied that
this was not a feint on the part of the enemy, but a serious
and determined attack, he ordered the troops to act on the
defensive; and after sending orders for his Second Brigade
to report, General Hartranft turned to inspect other portions of his lines.

General Hartranft[1] says : " Fortunately, upon the line
taken, the enemy could not easily deploy for the further
advance to Meade Station and the railroad, the enfilading
fires of Battery Nine and Fort Haskell forcing their troops
into the bomb-proofs of the captured lines to the right and
left of Fort Stedman, which were thus the only openings

---

[1] General Hartranft in Philadelphia "Press," March 17, 1886.

for their columns to enter and deploy to the rear. Great credit is justly due to the garrisons of these two points for their steadiness in holding them in the confusion and nervousness of a night attack. If they had been lost, the enemy would have had sufficient safe ground on which to recover and form their ranks, and the Third Division would have been overwhelmed and beaten in detail by a greatly superior force. . . . The tenacity with which these points were held, therefore, saved the Union army great loss of men, material, and time, and enabled the Third Division to signalize itself by a brilliant feat of arms."

In the check given the enemy at this point, where occurred the fiercest fighting of the day, General Hartranft received the active coöperation of the Eleventh Massachusetts Light Battery, commanded by Major E. J. Jones, stationed in Fort Friend, between the Dunn House Battery and General Willcox's headquarters. This battery had been relieved from duty in Fort McGilvery only the night before, for three days' rest in the rear, and did not get into position until nearly midnight. Major Jones informs the writer that before daylight some of the Union troops had aroused him with the information that the enemy had broken through the lines, bringing in at the same time five prisoners as proof of their statements. These prisoners he placed for a time in the ditch under guard, but afterwards sent them to General Willcox with the information they had communicated. He then took his guns out of Fort Friend, placed them on the edge of the ravine, and depressed them to such an angle as would permit him to hurl canister into the advancing column of the enemy. From his commanding position his fire did great execution, and he continued to pour fire into and around Fort Stedman upon any body of the enemy which made its appearance. Soon afterwards two guns of the Nineteenth New York Light Battery, and two of Battery G, First New York Artillery, were put in position on his immediate left, and coöperated with him in covering the troops.

The advances of the enemy to our right and rear having been checked, let us now follow the movements of the third column, which, after the capture of Fort Stedman, as we have seen, turned down the left and rear of the Union lines. About daylight this column advanced for the second time, according to the report of the commanding officer of the Twenty-ninth Massachusetts, attacking that portion of the regiment which had been deployed in rear of Battery Eleven, in front, flank, and rear, in such overwhelming force that those who were not captured made their escape toward Fort Haskell. The enemy next encountered the Fifty-ninth Massachusetts, which, according to General McLaughlin's statement, before quoted, was placed in Battery Eleven after the Twenty-ninth Massachusetts had been driven out in the first attack. The commanding officer of the Fifty-ninth[1] reports that when he was ordered to take possession of Battery Eleven it was

---

[1] Major Ezra P. Gould. Massachusetts Adjutant-General's Report, 1865.

done with but little difficulty, as the enemy had left the place apparently in search of larger game. But on going out very soon after in search of General McLaughlin (who had been captured), he found that the lines on either side of him were deserted, while the enemy, in a long line, completely outflanking his position, were advancing in his rear. It was a critical moment, and there was only one escape, and by his orders the regiment leaped over the breastworks in front and retreated between the enemy's lines and our own to Fort Haskell.

Continuing the attack toward the Union left, the enemy next came in contact with the One Hundredth Pennsylvania Volunteers, a veteran, and particularly gallant, regiment. This regiment, or a portion of it, was quickly drawn out of the trenches and deployed perpendicularly to the main line, to check the advancing enemy, who was now bent on the capture of Fort Haskell. The fight was hot and bloody, and Lieutenant-Colonel Pentecost, commanding the regiment, was killed. The greater portion of the Third Brigade, located on the right of Fort Haskell, which had escaped capture, had, by this time, retired to Fort Haskell, which now had a strong force in addition to the regular garrison, made up of the remnant of the brigade which had taken refuge there.

In the meantime, as we have seen, the Two Hundred and Eighth Pennsylvania, of Hartranft's Division, with Colonel Diven, the brigade commander, had gone from its camp near the Avery House to General McLaughlin's

headquarters, where it was placed in a good position
facing northward, at nearly a right angle with the main
line on the right of headquarters, the left resting within
one hundred yards of Fort Haskell, between which and
the Two Hundred and Eighth Regiment had been placed
two detachments of McLaughlin's brigade, numbering
about two hundred in all, including a portion of the
One Hundredth Pennsylvania and the Third Maryland,
making the line continuous to Fort Haskell.[1] The Two
Hundred and Eighth Regiment, upon arriving on the
ground, discovered the enemy, and immediately fired two
or three well-directed volleys, causing him to fall back
in some confusion to the cover of a ravine. The regiment
then advanced and drove him out of the ravine to the
cover of Battery Twelve and the lines of works connecting it with Fort Stedman, capturing about one
hundred prisoners. Reinforcements from the remainder of
the Third Brigade, now commanded by Colonel Robinson,
Third Maryland Volunteers, were soon brought into line
from the left of Fort Haskell, and the line was subsequently reinforced by a second line, consisting of the
One Hundred and Ninth New York and Thirty-seventh

---

[1] After placing the Two Hundred and Eighth Regiment in position, Captain
Prosper Dalien, Two Hundred and Eighth Regiment, engineer on the staff of
General Hartranft, in attempting to join the General, received a mortal wound.
He was an officer of much experience and promise. A native of France, he was
educated at the Military School at St. Cyr, and served throughout the Italian
war as lieutenant of cavalry. He was brevetted captain, and presented by
Napoleon III. with two medals for gallant conduct at Solferino.

Wisconsin, from Colonel Harriman's (First) Brigade, in obedience to standing orders that in the event of the line being broken at any point the brigade commanders should take out troops where they could best be spared from their respective fronts, and attack the flanks of the enemy.

The enemy made three attacks to obtain possession of Fort Haskell, which were handsomely repulsed by the garrison and the troops in the rear. The force in Fort Haskell was large, and the men who could not get into position to fire, loaded the muskets and passed them to those who stood along the parapet as fast as they could be fired. A lieutenant of the One Hundredth Pennsylvania states that he fired more than one hundred and fifty shots in a few minutes during the assaults. Thus a steady, well-directed fire of musketry was kept up, while the Third New Jersey Light Battery and First Connecti-

NOTE.—Major R. C. Eden, Thirty-seventh Regiment, Wisconsin Volunteers (First Brigade, First Division, Ninth A. C.), in History of that regiment, page 44 *et seq.*, says: "On the morning of the 25th of March we were aroused by the sound of three shots fired in rapid succession from the rebel lines. . . . Meantime the batteries on either side had opened, and were keeping up a very lively interchange of missiles; close on our right the second brigade was evidently warmly engaged. . . . After a few minutes we were ordered to the right of the brigade, and drawn up on the flank, at right angles to the main line of works. . . . Right in our front, on an eminence on the opposite side of a ravine, was Fort Stedman. In and around this a fierce fight was going on, and to the rear of it were to be seen flashes, indicating that sharp skirmishing was going on in the direction of Meade Station. The truth was at once apparent, . . . the enemy was now pushing for the City Point Railroad, and, perhaps, City Point itself; in fact, *our lines were broken.*"

cut Heavy Artillery inflicted great loss upon the enemy.
The attacks having been repulsed, the enemy slowly
retired along the line of trenches which he had captured,
and proceeded to plunder the camps, finding generous
rations of meat, coffee, bread, and sugar, which for months
had been sadly needed. He was not, however, permitted
to enjoy this luxury for any considerable time or to withdraw without molestation; for soon the troops from and
in rear of Fort Haskell moved forward, firing heavy
volleys, and pushed steadily through the trenches, all
uniting in driving him slowly but surely toward Fort
Stedman.[1]

Meanwhile Hartranft's Second Brigade had not been
idle. From its camp on the left, three to four miles
distant from the scene of action, it had hurried on the
double-quick to the Avery House, and at the very moment
when General Hartranft had concluded that its presence
was demanded, two regiments — the Two Hundred and
Fifth and Two Hundred and Seventh Pennsylvania —
were being conducted through a ravine running northward from the Avery House to a point directly in rear of

---

[1] Narratives of the action in and around Fort Haskell have been written
by Lieut. James H. Stevenson, One Hundredth Pennsylvania Volunteers, and
George L. Kilmer, Fourteenth New York Heavy Artillery. The former was
published in the Newcastle (Penn.) "Courant," 1885; the latter, in "The Cen-
tury Magazine," September, 1887. While these narratives contain interesting and
vivid descriptions of the battle at this point, it is evident that the writers were
entirely unaware of the serious nature of the conflict on the right of Fort Stedman,
or the desperate fighting by the troops of the Third Division in its rear.

Fort Stedman, entirely unobserved by the enemy, and took position under an abrupt bank which, though near the enemy, completely sheltered them from his fire.

The other regiment of this brigade, the Two Hundred and Eleventh Pennsylvania, on account of the greater distance of its camp from the rear of Fort Stedman, was last in reaching the ground, and was placed in position on the high land covering Meade Station, and in support of the artillery.

The situation at this time — 7.30 A.M. — was as follows : Batteries Eleven and Twelve had been regained, and a cordon of troops had been drawn around the rear of Fort Stedman and Battery Ten, forcing the masses of the enemy back into those works, where they were exposed to, and suffered greatly from, a concentrated fire from all the artillery in position bearing upon those points, and from the batteries on the hill in the rear. This fire covered the space in front of the enemy's lines with such a shower of missiles as to prevent any effort on his part to reinforce the attacking columns, and render any attempt at escape extremely hazardous. The cordon of troops was composed of Hartranft's Division and that portion of Willcox's Division which had formed at right angles with the entrenchments. The troops on the Union left faced nearly northward, those on the right nearly south, while Hartranft's Second Brigade, as yet undiscovered by the enemy, and the Two Hundredth Regiment, faced nearly westward. "Thus were formed," says General Hartranft, "two solid wing dams to check the enemy from sweeping the lines in the rear to the north or south. There was still a distance of three hundred yards between the left of the Two Hundredth and the right of the Two Hundred and Fifth, through which ran the road to Meade Station, uncovered; but any further advance of the enemy in that direction was impossible."

General Hartranft also says: " The time and opportunity to make these dispositions, were due entirely to the stubborn courage of the Two Hundredth Regiment. Lieut.-Colonel McCall had reason to be proud of the regiment he handled that morning so gallantly and skilfully. Its courage and steadiness undoubtedly saved that part of the army severe punishment. It is reported that the Duke of Wellington said that his test of a soldier was not whether he would run, but whether he would run and come back. Here were troops never before in action, who not only rallied promptly within fifty yards of where a concentric fire of artillery and musketry had broken them, but had resolutely recharged and held an advanced position for twenty minutes, and when fairly forced back by superior weight, re-rallied promptly on the first available ground. No veterans could have done better. Although they did not know it at the time, and were apparently awaiting the attack of a superior force, they had captured Fort Stedman in that twenty minutes' fight. The brave fellows who lay around the camp of the Fifty-seventh Massachusetts had not fallen in vain."

At 7.30 A.M. General Hartranft received an order to retake the lines. His plan of attack was instantly adopted. Orders were sent out that an assault would be made by the whole division in fifteen minutes, and that the signal of the charge would be the advance of the Two Hundred and Eleventh Regiment from the hill in the rear toward Fort Stedman, in line of battle in full view of the enemy. This was done with the intention and expectation of attracting the attention and drawing the fire of the enemy, and cover the movement of the remainder of the force which was to carry the works. Fort Stedman was now literally swarming with the enemy, who crowded parapets, bomb-proofs, and trenches. The ruse was a complete success. The enemy, seeing the advance of this regiment, numbering about six hundred muskets, in such handsome and gallant style, began to waver; and the remainder of the troops, responding to the signal, rose to the charge with a will. With loud cheers and in a most gallant manner they sprang from the ravine, where some had been secreted, and from the lines they had so courageously held, troops of the First and Third Divisions together, and dashed forward. Artillery and musketry opened upon them; but the enemy was brushed away in disorder, and in another moment Fort Stedman and the batteries, and the entire lines which had been lost, were recaptured, and the Stars and Stripes once more proudly floated where but a few moments before the Stars and Bars had so defiantly waved.

After the troops had commenced moving to make the assault, General Hartranft received orders not to make it until a division of the Sixth Corps, which was on its way to support him, had arrived; but he saw that success was certain, and it was doubtful if he could have communicated with the regiments on the flanks in time to countermand the order. He therefore allowed the line to charge.

As early as half-past six o'clock General Parke had ordered the Provisional Brigade at army headquarters to report to him, and directed General Warren to move the Fifth Corps in the direction of Fort Stedman. General Wright, at his direction, had ordered the division of General Wheaton to move to the threatened point. He moved promptly, but about the time he reached Ninth Corps headquarters the line had been recaptured.

In all the operations of the morning valuable and distinguished services were rendered General Hartranft by the various officers of the Ninth Corps Staff, prominent among whom, on that occasion, were Generals Charles G. Loring and Van Buren, and Colonel R. H. I. Goddard. Colonel Thomas Wm. Clarke, Adjutant General to General McLaughlin, Major Levi C. Brackett, Aide-de-camp to General Willcox, and Major George Shorkley, Assistant Inspector-General, Third Division (who was severely wounded), rendered conspicuous and gallant service. During the final attack Colonel Diven, commanding the First Brigade of Third Division, was wounded, and the command of the brigade devolved upon Lieutenant-

Colonel Wm. H. H. McCall, Two Hundredth Pennsylvania.

The trophies of the brilliant victory at Fort Stedman were one thousand nine hundred and forty-nine prisoners, including seventy-one commissioned officers, nine stands of colors, and a very large number of small-arms. On the Union side not a color or a piece of artillery was lost. All the guns in the lines were recaptured. One Coehorn mortar had been taken over the parapet of Battery Ten, and carried as far as the Union picket line and there abandoned.

The loss of the enemy has never been officially reported. That it was very heavy, there can be no doubt. General Grimes, who commanded Gordon's leading division, reports in his published letters a loss of four hundred and seventy-eight in his division alone. Captain Phisterer, in the "Statistical Record," Vol. XIII., Scribner's "Campaigns of the Civil War," p. 218, states the loss of the enemy — killed, wounded, and missing — to be two thousand six hundred and eighty-one.

Soon after the recapture of the lines, Major H. Kyd Douglass, General Gordon's adjutant-general, appeared in front of Fort Stedman with a flag of truce to ask permission to remove the Confederate dead from the space between the lines. The request was granted; and a truce prevailed nearly all day on that portion of the lines, during which one hundred and twenty dead and fifteen badly wounded lying between the lines were removed by the enemy.

The Union loss, officially reported, was as follows : —

FIRST DIVISION.

	Killed.	Wounded.	Missing.	Total.
Second Brigade	4	26	19	49
Third Brigade	34	135	430	599
	38	161	449	648

THIRD DIVISION.

	Killed.	Wounded.	Missing.	Total.
First Brigade	23	197	—	220
Second Brigade	2	36	—	38
	25	223	——	258

	Killed.	Wounded.	Missing.	Total.
Batteries in the lines	10	21	60	91
Artillery Brigade	2	4	14	20

AGGREGATE. — Killed, 75; Wounded, 419; Missing, 523; Total, 1,017.[1]

It may be regarded as an incident worthy of record that the final victorious charge of the troops was witnessed by President Lincoln from the high ground near the Dunn

[1] Captain Phisterer, in the volume referred to, reports the number of battles during the Civil War to be 2,261. In one hundred and forty-nine the total loss was five hundred or more on the side of the Union troops. In this number the battle of Fort Stedman ranks as ninety-one, the Union loss being stated to be nine hundred and eleven. The loss as officially reported, however, was one thousand and seventeen, which raises its rank to number eighty-two. In some of the battles where the Union loss is reported to be greater than that at Stedman, the casualties are given approximately, or in round numbers, or cover a series of engagements, as cavalry raids, etc. Omitting these, the place of Stedman in the list of the battles where the loss is precisely stated is seventy-seven.

In but forty-three of the battles in which the casualties of the Confederates are stated do their losses exceed the number reported at Fort Stedman (2,681).

House Battery. He had passed the previous night at City Point with Generals Grant and Meade, and a review had been arranged in honor of his visit to the army. The attack of the enemy at Stedman, and the subsequent advance of the Union lines on the left, rendered a change of programme necessary. While intently watching the surging charge of Hartranft's line, he is reported to have said, "This is better than a review." Later in the day, however, he was honored with a review. The Fifth Corps had been removed from its camp and sent over to the right, to be available for the support of the Ninth. Its services not being required, it was returning, and was halted for review by the President. That being over, it was hurried to the left, where General Wright was just then receiving a counter-attack from the enemy. "Thus, at nearly the same time, our lines presented the curious picture of a battle won and a truce prevailing on the right, a review in rear of the centre, and a severe engagement at the left."

Of all the gallant officers and men who performed their duty faithfully and well on that memorable morning, and of those who fought their last battle and sealed their devotion to the nation's cause with their blood, it is impossible to speak. And yet it may not be deemed invidious praise to mention one who particularly distinguished himself under most trying circumstances. While refraining from criticism, censure, or praise of the action of others, we but record accepted fact in the statement that the special

honors of the battle were worthily won and generously
bestowed upon General Hartranft, the commander of the
Third Division. General Parke says : " General Hartranft, to whom I had confided the task of recapturing the
fort, made his dispositions with great coolness and skill.
.   .   .   Too much credit cannot be given for the
skill in handling his division and gallantry in leading it
displayed by him." In this action he exhibited upon
the dark background of disaster the brilliant qualities
he had previously displayed on many a bloody field. He
was equal to the great emergency, and manifested not
only the military skill requisite to the command of a
large division, but the nerve to fight a single regiment
and lead it into the hottest fire. But for his oppor-
tune arrival in front of the Dunn House Battery with
the Two Hundredth Regiment, just in season to check
the advance of the enemy's line, it is impossible to state
what might have been the result. His fierce attack
upon the head of the enemy's column prevented its deployment, and gave time for the regiments on the right and
left to take strong positions. Had the enemy succeeded
in gaining the high ground in rear of our main lines, the
sequel of that morning's assault would have been far dif-
ferent. That this opinion was shared by his commanders
may be judged from their subsequent action. Immediately
after the battle General Parke recommended that General
Hartranft be brevetted Major-General, for ability and gallantry displayed that day. General Meade replied that he

had already forwarded a similar recommendation, and that his request for this special honor had been anticipated by General Grant and the Secretary of War. He received at once the reward so nobly won, and the act of justice was applauded by the entire army.

General orders were issued by General Meade congratulating General Parke on the prompt measures taken by him, praising the firm bearing of the troops of the Ninth Corps in the adjacent portions of the lines broken by the enemy, and the conspicuous bravery of the Third Division, for the first time under fire, together with the energy and skill displayed by General Hartranft, which quickly repaired a serious disaster and drove the enemy from our lines with heavy losses.

Thus was Stedman recovered, the last desperate thrust of the Confederate army successfully parried, and the disaster of the Mine avenged! Nine days later the Stars and Stripes waved over Petersburg and Richmond, and in six days more, at Appomattox Court House, seventy-seven miles west of Petersburg, on Palm Sunday, April 9, at 3.30 P.M., the Army of Northern Virginia surrendered. Fifteen days from Stedman to Appomattox! On the morning of the twenty-fifth of March, what prophetic eye beheld that vision? Is it possible that the great commander of the Union armies, in his profoundest anticipations, — "forecasting how his foe he might annoy," — could trace the brilliant pathway which led to such gigantic results?